Barbecue

Written by Quentin Flynn
Illustrated by Bettina Guthridge

Contents

1 Don't Panic! 4
2 A Meaty Expedition 12
3 Tools, Tools, Tools 24
4 Everything Under Control 31
5 Chicken or Turkey? 40

For learning solutions, visit cengage.com.au

Meet the Characters

Scarlett

An eleven-year-old girl (and the narrator).

Richard

Scarlett's hapless father.

Marcy

Scarlett's patient mother.

Jasper

Scarlett's cheeky brother.

TRIFFIC

The Turbo-Rotisserie-Ignition-Flame-Fired-Interactive-Cooker (or barbecue).

Dear Reader

One recent morning, I woke up to find that there was a power cut. There was no electricity, and that meant no toast and no coffee for breakfast. It was a disaster! Suddenly, I had an idea. I shuffled outside, in my pyjamas, and lit the barbecue. It took ages to make breakfast on it, but while I was waiting, I had an idea for a book. I hope you like it!

Quentin Flynn
Author

Our Street

1. A delivery truck
2. Our barbecue area
3. Our house
4. The neighbours

 Don't Panic!

I'd never seen Dad leap to his feet so quickly. The roast he was cooking as a surprise for Mum's birthday had burst into flames, and, within seconds, he'd sprayed the oven, the bench and the entire kitchen with the fire extinguisher.

"Don't panic, don't panic!" he shouted. "Everything's under control!"

Which, of course, it wasn't.

"Richard, dear, you're supposed to take the roast out of the plastic tray before you put it in the oven," coughed Mum, choking in the mixture of burnt-meat, melted-plastic and fire-extinguisher fumes.

Dad gave the kitchen bench another burst from the fire extinguisher, blasting the row of herbs off the windowsill with a loud crash.

"Emergency over!" called Dad, slipping in the greasy foam that covered the floor. With a pair of oven mitts, he rescued the smoking roast and ran it under the cold tap.

"Richard, you're not seriously thinking that ..." said Mum in an incredulous voice.

"Marcy, it'll be fine," smiled Dad. "The melted plastic will have sealed in the flavour! Won't it, Scarlett?"

Dad looked at me for support. I raised an eyebrow.

"Happy birthday, Mum," I said.

After three weeks, the smell still hadn't quite gone away. But each meal we cooked had less of the charred, plasticky, extinguisher-like flavour – "exotic", Dad called it.

That's when Dad ordered the new barbecue he'd seen on TV.

"You spent *how* much?" said Mum, when she found out.

"It's not how much I spent that counts," explained Dad. "It's how much I *saved*."

Mum sighed. She knew she was beaten. She'd used that line herself.

"At least now you know that Dad does listen to you," piped up my brother Jasper.

"And I also got a free set of steak knives, a steam mop and a new exercise machine to trim and tone tummy muscles," said Dad proudly. "You have been getting a little wide around the middle, dear," he said, winking.

Mum hadn't talked to him for a week after that. She went off to work each morning without a word. Dad cultivated the look of someone who had been accused of a dreadful crime, even though they were innocent, and should instead be in line for a sainthood.

Until the barbecue was delivered, that is. The knock on the door caused Dad to leap to his feet excitedly. He'd been looking forward to the delivery for days.

"Sign here," said the delivery driver when Dad flung open the front door. He sniffed. "Smells like you've been practising inside," grinned the driver. "Now you'll be able to barbecue to your heart's content outside!"

"No, no," said Dad sheepishly. "That was my wife's birthday."

"Must have been a lot of candles on that cake," observed the driver, wrinkling his nose.

The driver went back to his truck, with Dad, Jasper and me following. He pressed a button on the rear of the truck. The steel platform at the back lowered a huge cardboard box to the ground.

"Hey, Scarlett," said Jasper mischievously. "Dad's got himself a cardboard box to sleep in. Now we can have the couch back."

Dad was too busy staring at his new delivery to take any notice of Jasper. He was like a kid, eager to tear the wrapping paper off his present.

"I've also got these," called out the driver. He pointed to three more boxes in the truck. "Where would you like them?"

"Er, I don't think I'll need the exercise machine," replied Dad wisely. "But I will take the steam mop and steak knives!"

Dad put the cardboard box on a trolley and wheeled it around to the back. You could tell Dad was dying to snip the blue plastic straps that bound the cardboard in place and admire his new prize – but he knew he had to make things up with Mum first.

"Are you sure, Dad?" I said, when he told me what he was going to do.

"She'll love it, Scarlett," he grinned confidently. "What woman could resist a thoughtful gift like that?"

"OK, Dad," I said, making a mental note to be upstairs, in my room, with the door closed, when Mum came home from work. But of course I wasn't. Jasper and I couldn't resist watching this lovely gesture.

"Well, thank you, dear," smiled Mum when Dad handed over the gift he'd carefully wrapped in paper covered with pictures of soppy hearts and kissing teddy bears. "That's very sweet of you."

Dad nodded. He thought so, too.

"I'm sorry I snapped at you, Richard," she continued, pulling off a strip of wrapping paper. "I guess I ..."

2 A Meaty Expedition

Mum stopped. Dad winked at Jasper and me. I looked at the ceiling. Jasper looked at the floor. Mum looked at Dad.

"A steam mop," she said.

"It'll save you hours of back-breaking work around the house," said Dad.

"Yes, it will," replied Mum. Her face turned thunderously dark. "In fact, not just hours," she said. "Days. Weeks. Months."

Dad looked puzzled.

"So you'd better get started now!" said Mum, in a voice she usually reserved for people who held up supermarket queues by paying in ten-cent pieces. She shoved the steam mop back into Dad's bewildered arms and breezed off.

"Kitchen floor needs doing first," she called back. "Then the upstairs bathroom. Then the downstairs bathroom. Then ..."

I didn't quite catch what she said next, but if it was what I thought she said, I doubted Dad would manage that. It would be far too painful.

"Lucky you didn't give her the steak knives," piped up Jasper. "Then we *really* would have needed the steam mop to clean up the mess."

Mum didn't stay mad at Dad for long, of course. How could she, when he spent the entire next day steam-mopping the floors, the carpets, the windows, the couch, the dog and quite a bit of the wallpaper?

"We can paste it back on," she said, when the damp wallpaper started to peel off the wall.

Dad smiled weakly. "At least if it all falls off, there's a nice retro pattern underneath," he said. "Sorry. I didn't mean to get carried away."

"I don't mind you being carried away, Richard," said Mum sweetly. "In fact, I think you should get carried away more often."

"Really?" said Dad.

"Yes," said Mum, narrowing her eyes. "In an ambulance, tied up in a straitjacket, with large men in white coats."

Jasper and I snorted with laughter. Dad nodded resignedly.

"Well, before that happens, let's have at least one barbecue," he said brightly. "I'm going to unpack the TRIFFIC and cook dinner tonight."

TRIFFIC – that was the name of the barbecue Dad had bought, standing for Turbo-Rotisserie-Ignition-Flame-Fired-Interactive-Cooker. All seven of those words, in Dad's hands, were an invitation to disaster, but we all just smiled. We had to let Dad play with his new toy. If we didn't, he'd spend the weekend steam cleaning the lawns and Mum's vegetable patch. That wouldn't turn out well.

"Who's coming to the supermarket with me?" he said. "Come on, Scarlett. Come on, Jasper. Let's find ourselves a feast to cook for dinner."

Dad, Jasper and I headed for the car and pulled on our seatbelts. As Dad reversed down the driveway, Mum waved at us from the front step.

"Have a nice time," she said. "Don't forget to ask them if you can have your meat without plastic trays."

"I've never seen so much meat," said Jasper incredulously.

"Are you sure we're going to need all this?" I asked, as I tried to keep the supermarket trolley moving. Dad was perusing the meat aisle, stopping now and again to toss another package into the trolley.

"Don't worry," said Dad, who was reading the cooking instructions on a large pack of chicken offal. "Hmm, pretty sure these will just fall down the grate." He put the pack back. Jasper and I breathed a sigh of relief.

"Kids, TRIFFIC comes complete with six turbo burners, a hotplate, a self-cleaning mini-oven and a metre-long rotisserie," he said, sounding just like the TV ad. "And tonight we're going to see just what that baby's capable of!"

I looked at the brimming trolley.

Lamb cutlets, prawn cutlets, veal cutlets. Rump steak, T-bone steak, ham steak. Chicken fillets, salmon fillets, pork fillets. Spanish sausages, Chinese sausages, Italian sausages. A duck, a giant blue crab and a bright orange crayfish.

I already knew just what that baby was capable of – giving us all a mighty tummy ache.

"Dad, it's not healthy to eat all that meat," I said, shaking my head dubiously.

"You're right," said Dad, nodding seriously. He placed a small sprig of parsley on top of the trolley. "Mustn't forget the vegetables," he said.

I struggled to steer the trolley towards a checkout. Like an old car dripping oil, the trolley left a wobbly trail of blood drops marking our route away from the meat aisle.

"I'll tell the butcher to just give you a whole animal next time," joked the checkout girl drily. "Then you could just walk it out, rather than having to push it."

"Ha, ha," I said. Dad looked like he was considering the idea.

He was surprised when the total amount came up on the cash register. "Crikey!" he exclaimed. "Better take it easy on the parsley next time," he said, waggling a finger at me.

We arrived home. The boot was laden with leaking, dripping trays of meat and seafood.

Mum watched in amazement as we trudged inside with cutlets, steak, fillets, sausages, a duck, a giant blue crab and a bright orange crayfish.

"Is there anything left for anyone else in town to eat?" she asked, as we cleared space in the spare refrigerator in the garage.

"Look!" said Dad, ignoring Mum's question as he took a bottle out of the refrigerator. "This old bottle of milk has turned into cheese! Isn't that cool?" He unscrewed the lid, sniffed and staggered backwards.

"Blue cheese," he declared, after he got his breath back.

Mum shook her head and muttered something about Dad getting carried away again. Jasper, Dad and I packed the refrigerator and squeezed the door shut.

"Right!" announced Dad. "That's the barbecue food all sorted. Now we need to go to the local hardware store."

"The hardware store," repeated Jasper. "Why do we need to go there?"

"Because we are *real* men," replied Dad, folding his arms. "And *real* men need barbecue tools. Of course, that includes you, too, Scarlett," he added.

"Thanks, Dad," I said, trying not to sound too excited at the prospect of being transformed into a "real man".

We trooped back to the car. Mum watched us patiently from the step once more.

"Don't forget to get ..." she started.

"Ha, ha, ha," said Dad, waving cheerily as he reversed down the driveway. "Yes, dear, we've already heard that joke!"

Mum smiled and shook her head.

We headed for the hardware store.

3 Tools, Tools, Tools

"What kind of barbecue tools are you looking for?" asked the assistant.

Dad thought for a moment. He stroked his chin thoughtfully.

"Metal ones," he replied. "Metal ones with pointy bits."

"Ah," said the assistant, smiling at Jasper and me. "I see." She winked at me and turned back to Dad.

"In that case, you'll be needing the 'Real Man's Tools' aisle," she said. Dad's eyes lit up. He rubbed his hands together excitedly.

"Follow me," said the assistant.

"If you thought that supermarket trolley was heavy, you want to try pushing this," panted Jasper, straining to push the hardware-store trolley behind Dad. It turned out that real men needed all sorts of barbecue tools, not just metal pointy ones.

Dad was like a kid in a toyshop. After he chose a metal pointy tool, he decided he needed a metal sharp-edged tool, too. Then there was the metal steak-flipping tool, the metal sausage-puncturing tool and the metal grill-scraping tool.

"That grill-scraping tool is a bargain," said Dad. "It also has a bottle opener on the handle."

The contents of the trolley grew and grew. Real men needed chicken thermometers, fish-toasting cages and cast-iron oyster steamers (which, as Dad explained, could also double as snail poachers). There were extendable forks, extendable tongs and extendable skewers.

We had odd-shaped dishes for barbecuing quails, partridges and probably even small seagulls, if one was unlucky enough to end up at our place. We got an eel steamer and a haggis roaster, which Dad said Mum would be delighted with. Apparently we'd needed those for a long time.

Full-strength, grease-removing spray. Typhoon-resistant barbecue covers. Heat-repelling grill polish, as used on the space shuttle. A barbecue-tool belt, approved by the Fire-fighting Department. In it all went, until Jasper finally gave up.

"Dad, I can't move the trolley," he protested. "It's too heavy."

"Maybe they can lend us a forklift," I suggested.

Dad laughed. "What, for these few things?" he said jovially. "Anyway, that's all. Let's head to the checkout."

metal pointy TOOL
metal SHARP-EDGED TOOL
METAL STEAK-FLIPPING tool
METAL sausage-puncturing tool
metal GRILL-SCRAPING tool bottle OPENER
chicken thermometer
fish-toasting CAGE cast-iron oyster steamers
SNAIL POACHERS EXTENDABLE FORKS EXTENDABLE TONGS
extendable skewers dishes for barbecuing QUAILS, partridges and small seagulls EEL steamer
HAGGIS ROASTER full-strength
GREASE-removing spray typhoon-resistant
barbecue COVER heat-repelling grill polish
barbecue-tool BELT

He took over from Jasper and, even though he did look red in the face, he pushed the trolley almost all the way to the checkout before the front left wheel broke off, with a snap. It wobbled wildly up the tapware aisle.

It was two o'clock before we made it home. Twice, traffic officers stopped us. One wanted to know if Dad had a heavy-vehicle licence because it looked as though he needed one. The other insisted on Dad explaining why there was so much fresh blood in the boot.

He asked us if Dad had been acting strangely lately.

"No," said Jasper truthfully.

"It's been going on for a long time now," I added.

"Ever since he got the steak knives!" grinned Jasper. THAT added another half an hour to the police interview.

4 Everything Under Control

"You're sure you've got everything you need?" said Mum. Dad was busily marinating things, a process that took up the entire kitchen bench, the kitchen table and the ironing board. It also required every bowl and plastic container we owned.

"When you were going out before, I was about to tell you don't forget …" Mum went on.

"Of course we have everything," beamed Dad, wiping his hands on his apron. "Relax. Everything's under control."

The last time he'd said that was while he was extinguishing a flaming roast encased in a molten-plastic meat tray, so he shouldn't have been surprised when Mum didn't look entirely convinced.

"OK, I won't say another word," said Mum. She went and sat on the couch, passing the time flicking through the pages of her book.

Meanwhile, Dad used all the skills he had picked up from watching re-runs of cooking shows on TV. He diced, he sliced, he julienned. He chopped, crushed and carved. It was amazing to see.

Finally, as dusk fell outside, Dad was satisfied with his culinary efforts. He flapped a tea towel like a professional and looked extremely pleased with himself.

"Right, team," he announced, looking at Jasper and me. "I think we're just about ready to …"

Then it happened. At that very moment, there was a power cut.

The clocks on the oven and the microwave blinked and died. The CD playing on the stereo ground to a halt. The lights in the kitchen and the lounge flickered and went out. The whole house was plunged into shadow.

Mum got up off the couch and peered through the window.

"The street lights are off and all the neighbour's houses are dark, too," she said. "Looks like the electricity is out."

"Bother," I said. "And I was just about to go and do my homework on the computer." I sighed and tried my best to look disappointed.

"And I was just about to offer to do the vacuuming," said Jasper, shaking his head in dismay.

"Really?" said Mum in a voice that showed we needed to pay more attention during drama class.

"Well, at least we can still have dinner!" said Dad happily. "We don't need electricity for the TRIFFIC."

"And we can boil up a pot full of water for cups of hot chocolate afterwards," I said.

"And we can warm ourselves in front of the burners," said Jasper.

"And we can heat up some hot water for dishwashing, too," said Dad. "We can be fully self-sufficient! While everyone else in the street is wondering what to do with no power, we can be feasting on cutlets, steak, fillets, sausages, a duck, a giant blue crab and a bright orange crayfish!"

"Don't forget the parsley, Dad," I said.

"I won't," he smiled. "Just because there's a power cut, it doesn't mean we can't have a balanced and healthy diet!"

It was getting darker and darker outside. Mum suggested we fill the largest pots we could find with water before it got too dark to see inside. Fortunately, Dad hadn't used everything for marinating things. I helped Mum with the pots of water, while Jasper went to search for torches and candles.

"No telling how long the power cut will last," said Dad. "Just as well we're prepared," he added. "People will soon be smelling the delicious aroma of barbecuing food drifting across the street. Then they'll all be glum that they didn't get themselves a TRIFFIC, too!" he said proudly, glancing across at Mum. He still wasn't completely sure if she'd forgiven him for buying the barbecue off the TV, but this was really going to clinch the deal.

Like an elite, highly trained soldier, Dad unfurled the barbecue-tool belt he'd bought from the hardware store and strapped it firmly around his waist.

Then, he chose his weapons, determined he would be equipped to take on the worst that an exploding sausage could hurl at him.

"Metal pointy tool," Dad recited grimly.

"Check," said Jasper.

"Metal sharp-edged tool."

"Check."

"Metal steak-flipping tool."

"Check."

"Metal sausage-puncturing tool."

"Check."

"If we ever get attacked by invading smallgoods, I'm glad we'll be able to sleep soundly in our beds," sighed Mum, rolling her eyes.

Dad filled his pockets with a handful of oyster steamers, just in case he discovered a bed of oysters in the backyard, and grabbed the chicken thermometer.

"Let's roll," drawled Dad. He headed for the back door, clinking like a tin scarecrow.

"Five minutes," whispered Mum, winking at us. "Mark my words. Ten at the most."

Jasper and I looked at her, wondering what she meant.

In fact, it only took three minutes.

5 Chicken or Turkey?

Dad clanked his way back indoors, eyes downcast and looking crestfallen. This wasn't exactly how he'd planned to make his triumphant return, laden with the tasty spoils of victory.

"Yes, dear?" said Mum innocently. "Everything under control?"

"Gas," he said, looking forlornly at all of us. "I forgot to get some gas."

We all piled into the car. The last of the twilight had completely disappeared by now, and there was nothing anyone could do in the darkness of the house.

Jasper and I were in the back seat, watching Mum and Dad with amusement. They weren't saying anything, but we could tell by the looks on their faces what kind of conversation was going on in their heads.

"I did try to tell you," Mum would be thinking. "At least twice. But did you listen? Oh, no!"

"They should sell those barbecues with a gas bottle," Dad would be thinking, planning a letter of complaint to the barbecue company, the TV station and probably our local member of parliament.

Of course, they both just smiled at each other as Dad reversed down the driveway.

"We'll head to the local garage," said Dad cheerfully. "They'll have gas bottles. Within five minutes, we'll be back on track."

"Besides," Dad added, "another few minutes of marinating will make all that meat extra tender."

"Richard, if I didn't know you better, I'd say you cleverly planned all this to make sure our meat was extra tender," said Mum. Dad was busily peering at the darkened road ahead, so he didn't see Mum turn and wink at Jasper and me. But he did sit up a littler straighter, shoulders back, with a smile on his face.

"This seat's a little uncomfortable," commented Dad a couple of minutes later. He wriggled around. "Feels like one of the springs has come loose."

"Are you sure it's not a screw loose?" asked Mum.

We all burst out laughing, even Dad.

Dad's straight back and square shoulders did slump a little when we made it to the garage to find it well and truly closed. There's not a great deal of petrol pumping, tyre inflating or super-foamy car washing that can be done while there's a power cut.

"The power can't be out everywhere," said Mum. "Let's head over to Bankside and find a garage there."

Bankside was the next suburb and when we arrived there, it was a relief to see street lights, houses and shops all lit up.

Dad bought a full gas bottle at the very first garage we saw, and proudly carried it back to the car, giving us all the "thumbs up" sign. He leapt into the driver's seat and there was a loud crunching sound. Dad squirmed awkwardly.

Suddenly the car was filled with a shrill bleeping sound, like an alarm. Dad leapt out of his seat, and looked at the upholstery anxiously. Nothing. Then he patted his back trouser pocket and pulled out the chicken thermometer he'd been sitting on for the last half an hour.

"Good news," he announced as the thermometer let out a final fuzzy beep. "Apparently the chicken's ready!"

We all started laughing.

"Are you sure that's not for a turkey?" said Mum mischievously, and that kept us hooting and giggling all the way home.

I'd have to admit we had a great evening. Once it was hooked up to the gas bottle, TRIFFIC did a wonderful job sizzling its way through all the food that Dad had prepared. Mum went and invited the neighbours over, because there was no way we could have eaten everything ourselves, and soon the whole street was having a great time. Everybody brought deck chairs and candles and we all gathered around the barbecue chatting and laughing.

Dad was in his element, and looked for all the world like a proud sea captain at the helm of his ship. He handed out steak knives, flipped switches, adjusted knobs and wielded an array of barbecue tools like a ninja barbecue warrior who'd been doing it for years.

Afterwards, we all sat around doing traditional post-barbecue things, such as rubbing our tummies, groaning and undoing our belts a notch or two. The power came back on, but nobody was interested in going indoors. By the end of the evening, our neighbours waddled and groaned their way home, happy and contented. Soon, it was just me, Jasper, Mum and Dad again.

"That was delicious, dear," said Mum. "Well done. You had everything under control."

"I did, didn't I?" said Dad, sounding a little surprised. "And someone even managed to bring oysters for the oyster steamers. Wasn't that lucky? They were yummy!"

Jasper opened his mouth, but I nudged him before he could spoil Dad's good mood. There was no point in telling him that they weren't really oysters and that they'd actually been plucked off the bottom of Mum's cabbage plants.

"I think I ate too much," said Mum, yawning and clearing away the last of the dishes. "I think we'll all need to go on a diet tomorrow!" she added, patting her tummy.

"I can always ring up the delivery folks and get them to bring around the ... *ooof*!"

I nudged Dad, probably a little too hard, before he could spoil Mum's good mood. We didn't need the revolutionary new exercise machine to trim and tone tummy muscles.

"We can just have leftovers," I said smiling.

"Leftovers?" said Mum, Dad and Jasper together. "But we've eaten everything!"

"Not quite everything," I replied.

As usual, Dad had forgotten one thing. There it was, sitting on the kitchen bench, the leftovers from our TRIFFIC evening. Everybody laughed.

It was the sprig of parsley.